Rhino Horns

Anders Hanson

Illustrated by C.A. Nobens

Consulting Editor, Diane Craig, M.A./Reading Specialist

ABDO
Publishing Company

Published by ABDO Publishing Company, 4940 Viking Drive, Edina, Minnesota 55435.

Printed in the United States.

E Hanson

Credits
Edited by: Pam Price
Curriculum Coordinator: Nancy Tuminelly
Cover and Interior Design and Production: Mighty Media
Photo Credits: AbleStock, Corbis Images, Corel, Digital Vision, Philip Greenspun, ShutterStock

Library of Congress Cataloging-in-Publication Data

Hanson, Anders, 1980-
    Rhino horns / Anders Hanson ; illustrated by C.A. Nobens.
        p. cm. -- (Fact & fiction. Animal tales)
    Includes index.
    Summary: Randy Rhino, the biggest guy in school, puts on an unexpected show during the football game. Contains facts about rhinoceroses.
    ISBN 1-59679-963-3 (hardcover)
    ISBN 1-59679-964-1 (paperback)
    [1. Rhinoceroses --Fiction.] I. Nobens, C.A., ill. II. Title. III. Series.
    PZ7.H1982867Rhi 2006
    [E]--dc22
                                                                                2005024443

SandCastle Level: Fluent

SandCastle™ books are created by a professional team of educators, reading specialists, and content developers around five essential components—phonemic awareness, phonics, vocabulary, text comprehension, and fluency—to assist young readers as they develop reading skills and strategies and increase their general knowledge. All books are written, reviewed, and leveled for guided reading, early reading intervention, and Accelerated Reader® programs for use in shared, guided, and independent reading and writing activities to support a balanced approach to literacy instruction. The SandCastle™ series has four levels that correspond to early literacy development. The levels help teachers and parents select appropriate books for young readers.

| **Emerging Readers** | **Beginning Readers** | **Transitional Readers** | **Fluent Readers** |
| (no flags) | (1 flag) | (2 flags) | (3 flags) |

These levels are meant only as a guide. All levels are subject to change.

FACT & Fiction

This series provides early fluent readers the opportunity to develop reading comprehension strategies and increase fluency. These books are appropriate for guided, shared, and independent reading.

FACT The left-hand pages incorporate realistic photographs to enhance readers' understanding of informational text.

Fiction The right-hand pages engage readers with an entertaining, narrative story that is supported by whimsical illustrations.

The Fact and Fiction pages can be read separately to improve comprehension through questioning, predicting, making inferences, and summarizing. They can also be read side-by-side, in spreads, which encourages students to explore and examine different writing styles.

FACT OR **Fiction?** This fun quiz helps reinforce students' understanding of what is real and not real.

SPEED READ The text-only version of each section includes word-count rulers for fluency practice and assessment.

GLOSSARY Higher-level vocabulary and concepts are defined in the glossary.

SandCastle™ would like to hear from you.

Tell us your stories about reading this book. What was your favorite page? Was there something hard that you needed help with? Share the ups and downs of learning to read. To get posted on the ABDO Publishing Company Web site, send us an e-mail at:

sandcastle@abdopublishing.com

The white rhino is the second-largest land mammal. Only elephants are bigger than rhinos.

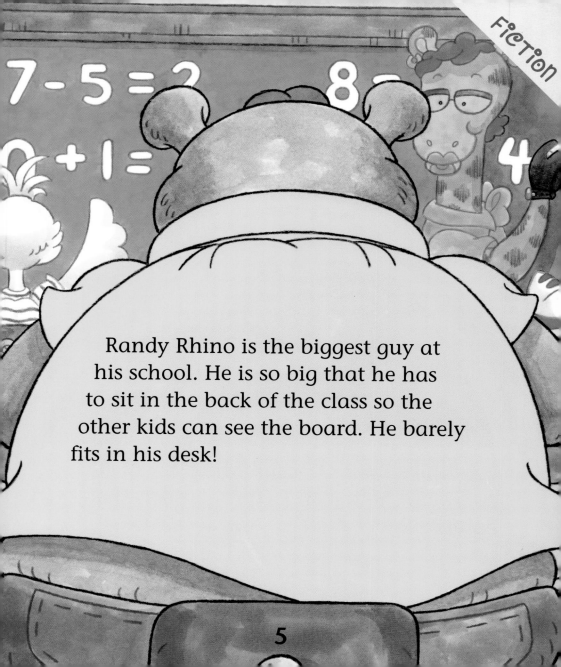

Randy Rhino is the biggest guy at his school. He is so big that he has to sit in the back of the class so the other kids can see the board. He barely fits in his desk!

Egrets like rhinos because their large feet churn up the soil and expose insects that egrets eat.

"I don't like being bigger than everyone else," Randy tells his friend Erik Egret, "but I love playing the tuba!" Playing horn in the band is Randy's chance to fit in with the other kids.

7

The five species of rhinos are Sumatran, Javan, black, white, and Indian. All five species are in danger of becoming extinct.

Tonight Randy is a bit nervous. The marching band is performing during their school's football game. "I know I'm going to mess up," he worries. "Everyone will see me because I'm so huge!"

Rhinos have excellent hearing. They can rotate their ears to focus on a sound.

Go Team!

As the band begins to march, Randy starts to relax. He even closes his eyes so he can hear himself play better. A moment later, he hears Erik squawking, "Randy? Randy? Where are you going?"

11

Although they usually move at a leisurely pace, rhinos can gallop for short distances at speeds up to 40 miles per hour.

Randy opens his eyes.
He realizes that he has
marched straight into
the middle of the
football game!

Randy squeals with embarrassment
and starts to run off the
field, but it's too late!
His team has
thrown him
the ball!

13

Rhinos can't see very well and sometimes accidentally attack trees or rocks.

Randy knows that his school is depending on him, so he charges blindly toward the football, puts his hands out, and jumps.

A rhino's horn is not bone. It is made of keratin, a substance found in human fingernails and hair.

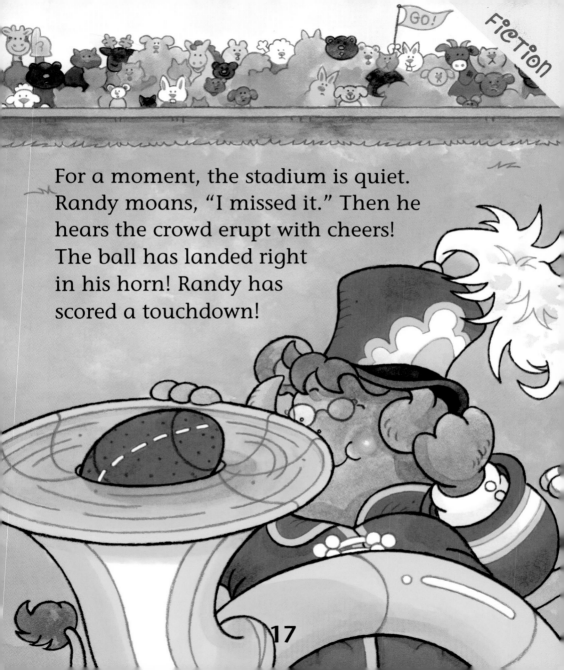

For a moment, the stadium is quiet. Randy moans, "I missed it." Then he hears the crowd erupt with cheers! The ball has landed right in his horn! Randy has scored a touchdown!

17

An adult white rhino can weigh over 5,000 pounds!